This Orchard
book belongs to

D0346868

For Benedicte Barford and Stephanie Amster
with love and thanks Emma

ORCHARD BOOKS

338 Euston Road, London NW1 3BH

Orchard Books Australia

Level 17/207 Kent Street, Sydney, NSW 2000

First published in 2009 by Orchard Books
First published in paperback in 2010

ISBN 978 1 84616 995 3

Text and illustrations © Emma Dodd 2009

The right of Emma Dodd to be identified as
the author and illustrator of this work
has been asserted by her in accordance
with the Copyright, Designs and
Patents Act, 1988.

A CIP catalogue record for this book
is available from the British Library.

10 9 8 7 6 5 4 3 2 1

Printed in China

Orchard Books is a division of
Hachette Children's Books,
an Hachette UK company.
www.hachette.co.uk

I don't want a cool cat

Emma Dodd

ORCHARD BOOKS

I don't want

want
a cool cat.

A treat-me-like-a-fool cat.

I don't want a stuffy cat.

A huffy, over-fluffy cat.

I don't want
a night cat.

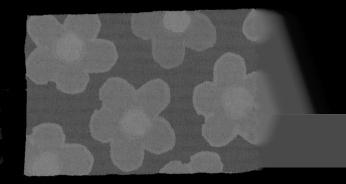

A looking-for-a-fight cat.

A glad

when

I come

home cat.

A cat I can call

My Own Cat.